For my mother, Carolyn Whitten Boston,
who taught me to pray
—C.B.W.

To Tiffani, we walk the walk so that your path would be clearer.
We talk the talk so the "no" we heard will become the "yes you can." Be good, be great. Love, Dad
—F.M.

Text copyright © 2022 by Carole Boston Weatherford
Jacket art and interior illustrations copyright © 2022 by Frank Morrison

All rights reserved. Published in the United States by Crown Books for Young Readers,
an imprint of Random House Children's Books, a division of
Penguin Random House LLC, New York.

Crown and the colophon are registered trademarks of
Penguin Random House LLC.

Visit us on the Web! rhcbooks.com
Educators and librarians, for a variety of teaching tools,
visit us at RHTeachersLibrarians.com

Library of Congress Cataloging-in-Publication Data is available upon request.
ISBN 978-0-593-30634-5 (trade) — ISBN 978-0-593-30635-2 (lib. bdg.) —
ISBN 978-0-593-30636-9 (ebook)

The text of this book is set in 14-point Sabon.
The illustrations were created using oil and spray paint on illustration board.
Book design by Nicole de las Heras

MANUFACTURED IN CHINA
10 9 8 7 6 5 4 3 2 1
First Edition

STANDING IN THE NEED OF PRAYER

A Modern Retelling of the Classic Spiritual

Written by
Carole Boston Weatherford

Illustrated by
Frank Morrison

Crown Books for Young Readers
New York

It's me, it's me, O Lord,
Standing in the need of prayer.
It's me, it's me, O Lord,
Standing in the need of prayer.

Not my father, not my mother,
but it's me, O Lord,
Standing in the need of prayer.
Not my father, not my mother,
but it's me, O Lord,
Standing in the need of prayer.

It's families enslaved and sold apart,
Standing in the need of prayer.
It's runaways fleeing the yoke by dark,
Standing in the need of prayer.

It's a preacher with a scar like a lightning bolt,
Standing in the need of prayer.
It's a band of rebels who are plotting revolt,
Standing in the need of prayer.

It's freedmen seeking kin at Emancipation,
Standing in the need of prayer.
It's millions on the move in the Great Migration,
Standing in the need of prayer.

It's Black troops tearing down
the color line,
Standing in the need of prayer.

It's brilliance onstage about to shine,
Standing in the need of prayer.

It's the first Black students walking into
    all-white classes,
Standing in the need of prayer.
It's orators, whose daring words
    move the masses,
Standing in the need of prayer.

It's churches hosting rallies and planning meetings,
Standing in the need of prayer.
It's marchers who brave insults, hate, slurs, and beatings,
Standing in the need of prayer.

It's record-breaking athletes who are
    so unreal,
Standing in the need of prayer.
It's champions-turned-warriors who,
    in protest, kneel,
Standing in the need of prayer.

It's choirs that sing of justice that
change will bring,
Standing in the need of prayer.
This land is both yours and mine,
let freedom ring.
Standing in the need of prayer.

Not my preacher, not my teacher, but it's me, O Lord,
Standing in the need of prayer.
Not my preacher, not my teacher, but it's me, O Lord,
Standing in the need of prayer.

It's me, it's me, O Lord,
Standing in the need of prayer.
It's me, it's me, O Lord,
Standing in the need of prayer.

It's me, it's me, O Lord,
Standing in the need of prayer.

REFERENCES

SLAVERY

In the seventeenth and eighteenth centuries, millions of Africans were brought to America in chains and forced into a life of slavery. They were made to work hard jobs for no pay and were denied basic freedoms. It's likely that slavery in North America started in 1619, when a ship brought African captives to Jamestown, Virginia. Most African descendants were enslaved on plantations in southern states, growing things like cotton and rice. It was difficult work, and many of the enslaved were treated cruelly by their masters.

NAT TURNER (1800–1831)

Some of the enslaved tried to rebel against their masters. Nathanial "Nat" Turner was an enslaved preacher who led the most effective slave rebellion in American history. He believed that he was chosen by God to lead his fellow slaves to freedom. In 1831, Nat Turner started a violent revolution, but it didn't end slavery. In fact, white slave owners were so scared by the rebellion that they made it even harder for Black people to get an education or travel.

THE AMERICAN CIVIL WAR (1861–1865)

Many Americans realized that slavery was wrong, and the abolition movement worked to end enslavement. The issue caused a growing conflict in the United States between states that supported slavery and states that opposed slavery. Eventually eleven southern states seceded from the United States to form the Confederate States of America. This sparked the American Civil War.

THE EMANCIPATION PROCLAMATION

Emancipation means setting someone free. When President Abraham Lincoln issued the Emancipation Proclamation in 1863, ending slavery became the focus of the Civil War. The proclamation freed about three million enslaved people in rebel states and convinced other countries to support the Union. Eventually, the Emancipation Proclamation paved the way for the prohibition, or end, of slavery.

THE GREAT MIGRATION

Even after slavery was made illegal, life was hard for Black people in America. Poverty and racism drove more than six million African Americans from their homes in the South to towns across America. Many headed to big cities like New York, Chicago, and Philadelphia, where there were more opportunities to find jobs and build communities.

THE TUSKEGEE AIRMEN

African Americans continued to face obstacles, such as segregation laws that denied them the same opportunities as white people. For example, many Black men wanted to join the armed forces, but racial segregation in the military prevented this. In 1939, President Franklin Roosevelt announced that the US Army Air Corps would start training Black pilots. Young men came from across the country to train at Tuskegee Army Air Field in Alabama. The Tuskegee Airmen fought bravely in World War II and helped win the war for the Allies. Their courage represented an important step toward American racial integration.

MUSIC

African Americans have been instrumental in the history of music. Many music genres have roots in African rhythms and African American spirituals that originated during slavery, including blues, jazz, funk, gospel, and hip-hop. Musicians and singers like Duke Ellington, Paul Robeson, Billie Holiday, Miles Davis, Louis Armstrong, and Nina Simone are just some of the brilliant artists who have influenced the world with their music.

RUBY BRIDGES (b. 1954)

In 1960, Ruby Bridges became the first Black student to attend the previously all-white William Frantz Elementary School in New Orleans, Louisiana. Federal marshals escorted Ruby and her mother in order to protect them from the angry mob that was waiting there. As soon as Ruby bravely entered the school, white parents pulled their children out, and all the teachers except for one refused to teach while a Black child was enrolled. Only one person agreed to teach Ruby, and for the entire school year, Ruby was the only student in her class.

MARTIN LUTHER KING JR. (1929–1968)

Almost one hundred years after slavery ended, the United States was still struggling with racial discrimination. This led to the Civil Rights Movement of the 1950s and '60s. Dr. Martin Luther King Jr. devoted his life to demanding equality and human rights for African Americans. Dr. King worked with civil rights and religious groups to organize huge peaceful protests that helped to end segregation and guaranteed important rights for Black Americans.

FLOJO (1959–1998)

One of many outstanding African American athletes, Florence Griffith Joyner ("FloJo") was known as the fastest woman in the world! She smashed world records at the Olympic Games and won gold medals for the United States.

COLIN KAEPERNICK (b. 1987)

Many famous Black Americans have used their status to raise awareness of important issues. Colin Kaepernick, a quarterback in the National Football League, knelt during the American national anthem in protest of police brutality and racial inequality. While some people criticized his actions as unpatriotic, many others praised him for protesting racism.

BLACK LIVES MATTER (founded in 2013)

America has come a long way since the days of slavery, but there is still a lot of work to be done. Black Americans continue to face intolerance and danger every day. The Black Lives Matter movement was born out of anger at police brutality and systemic discrimination against Black Americans. It has inspired protests around the globe from people who want a more just world.

ONLINE RESOURCES

history.com/topics/black-history/slavery • nationalgeographic.org/topics/resource-library-slavery
battlefields.org/learn/articles/brief-overview-american-civil-war • civilwar.com
history.com/topics/american-civil-war/american-civil-war-history
history.com/topics/american-civil-war/emancipation-proclamation
history.com/topics/black-history/great-migration
smithsonianmag.com/history/long-lasting-legacy-great-migration-180960118
history.com/topics/world-war-ii/tuskegee-airmen • tuskegeeairmen.org
music.si.edu/story/musical-crossroads
adl.org/education/resources/backgrounders/civil-rights-movement
history.com/topics/black-history/civil-rights-movement • biography.com/activist/martin-luther-king-jr
nobelprize.org/prizes/peace/1964/king/biographical
history.com/topics/black-history/central-high-school-integration
womenshistory.org/education-resources/biographies/ruby-bridges
biography.com/activist/ruby-bridges • biography.com/athlete/florence-joyner
espn.com/classic/biography/s/Griffith_Joyner_Florence.html
washingtonpost.com/sports/2020/06/01/colin-kaepernick-kneeling-history
biography.com/athlete/colin-kaepernick • blacklivesmatter.com
history.com/topics/black-history/black-history-milestones

AUTHOR'S NOTE

The African American spiritual, which is a type of religious folk song, originated with enslaved Black people in the South. The enslaved not only sang spirituals during worship but also while working in the fields. Some spirituals even passed along coded messages of pending escapes.

Created by and for enslaved people not allowed to read or write, many spirituals are in call-and-response style. The song leader sings a line of text, and the choir sings a refrain in unison. When so moved, singers improvise, adapting the existing lyrics or adding new ones. The text of this book was created in that same spirit, integrating historical and contemporary events that summoned courage and faith. It extends the lyrics of the beloved spiritual "Standing in the Need of Prayer," which is also known as "It's Me, It's Me, O Lord."

"Standing in the Need of Prayer" takes me back to the early 1990s, when I was a new mother toting my two children to the rural churches where their father was the minister. This song was a favorite at revivals and praise services. It also reminds me of my grandfather Lun Whitten, an activist minister in Appalachia during the Jim Crow era. This spiritual conjures my apron-wearing grandmothers, who hummed hymns as they went about household chores. And it makes me recall my mother, who taught me to pray, and my father, who ended each day kneeling at his bedside. Most of all, it brings back the times when I, as a mother, had nowhere to turn but to God. "Standing in the Need of Prayer" echoes my spirit.

This spiritual advocates a close, personal relationship with God—a bond forged through prayer. The song also elevates the concept of family, a core value among African Americans, who dreaded the separation that could come with enslavement. Most of all, it affirms the power of prayer. That power, as this hymn proclaims, is vital to anyone, to everyone, to you. However simple, prayers express inner feelings of joy, sadness, gratitude, grief, conflict, and compassion. And prayer is accessible to all.

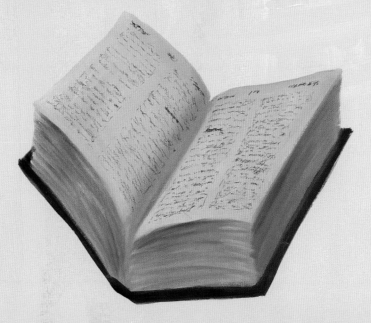